In the Town of Sweet Pickles, the animals get into and out of pickles because of their all too human personality traits.

Each of the books in the *Sweet Pickles* series is about a different pickle.

This book is about friends and borrowing and jumping to conclusions.

Library of Congress Cataloging in Publication Data

Hefter, Richard.
    Some friend.
    (Sweet Pickles)
    Summary: Walrus is so worried that Bear won't lend him a warm wooly hat that he develops hostile feelings for his friend before even asking for the favor.
    [1. Winter—Fiction. 2. Hats—Fiction. 3. Worry—Fiction] I. Perle, Ruth Lerner. II. Title.
PZ7.H3587So   [E]   81-15165
ISBN 0-937524-13-1   AACR2

Published by Euphrosyne, Inc.
Sweet Pickles is the registered trademark of Perle/Reinach/Hefter
Printed in the United States of America
Weekly Reader Books' Edition

Weekly Reader Books Presents

SOME FRIEND

Written and illustrated
by Richard Hefter

Edited by Ruth Lerner Perle

Euphrosyne Incorporated

It was a cold and wintery morning in the Town of
Sweet Pickles.

Worried Walrus was standing by the window,
looking out at all the snow on the ground.

"Oh, dear," he sighed. "Oh, my. This is a problem. I
have to be the starter at the sled race this afternoon
and I can't find my warm woolly hat."

Walrus looked in his closet again. He found his
tennis racket. He found his umbrella. He found his
water wings and his spare first-aid kit. But he didn't
find his warm woolly hat.

"I don't know what to do!" he groaned. "The race starts at three o'clock and it won't start without me because I'm supposed to start it and everyone knows you can't go out in the cold without a warm hat."

"I'm so worried," snuffled Walrus. "If I don't go to the race, everyone will be angry at me. If I *do* go to the race, and I *don't* wear a hat, I'm afraid I'll catch a terrible cold."

Walrus started to look through his drawers for the fifth time.

"There I'll be," moaned Walrus, "standing out in the cold, sniffling. Then the chills will start, and the sore throat, and the headache."

Walrus found his boots. He found his thick scratchy socks. He found his soft striped scarf and his thick mittens. But he didn't find his warm woolly hat.

"I can see it all now," he wailed. "I'm standing there on that freezing lonely hilltop with an awful cold in my head. The aches and pains are getting worse and worse. My dose is stuffed up ad there's dothing I cad do about it. I start to sneeze."

Walrus started to pace back and forth in his room.
"I can't do it!" he wailed. "I must have a woolly hat!
I won't go to the race without one."

Walrus tried to think of a way to get a woolly hat in time for the race. He thought about knitting one, but it would take too long. He thought about making a hat out of a paper bag but that wouldn't be warm enough. Then he thought about borrowing a warm woolly hat.

"That's it!" smiled Walrus. "I'll borrow a warm woolly hat from my best friend, Bashful Bear. Then I'll be able to go to the race."

Walrus put on his boots and his snow pants and an extra sweater. He pulled on his thick jacket and wrapped his soft striped scarf around his neck. Then he slipped his hands into his mittens and clumped out the door.

Walrus marched through the snow toward Bear's house.

"What a great idea!" mumbled Walrus as he crunched along. "Bear will lend me a hat. He's my friend. He's a terrific guy. Why, he'd lend me the shirt off his back!"

At the corner of Fifth and Main, Walrus stopped to catch his breath.

"Sure," he thought, "Bear will lend me his hat. He won't be going to the race anyway. He's too bashful. He wouldn't go unless someone invited him."

Walrus marched down Main Street. At the corner of Main and Center, he stopped again.

"Suppose someone invited Bear," grumbled Walrus. "Then he would want to wear his own hat to the race and he wouldn't lend it to me. Maybe Bear has an extra hat."

Walrus got to Sixth Street.

"And if Bear doesn't have an extra hat," grumped
Walrus, "and he wants to go to the race, then he
wouldn't lend his hat to me. Even though I'm his
best friend and I'm the starter for the race and the
whole thing is off without me."

"There I am," moaned Walrus, "stuck at home because I can't go out without a hat. And there's Bear at the race wearing his stupid old hat. And they give him the starter's job because I'm not there."

"Some friend!" scowled Walrus. "I ask for one simple favor and does he do it? No!"

Walrus marched past the bushes in front of Bear's house.

"Who would have thought that Bear would be so selfish!"

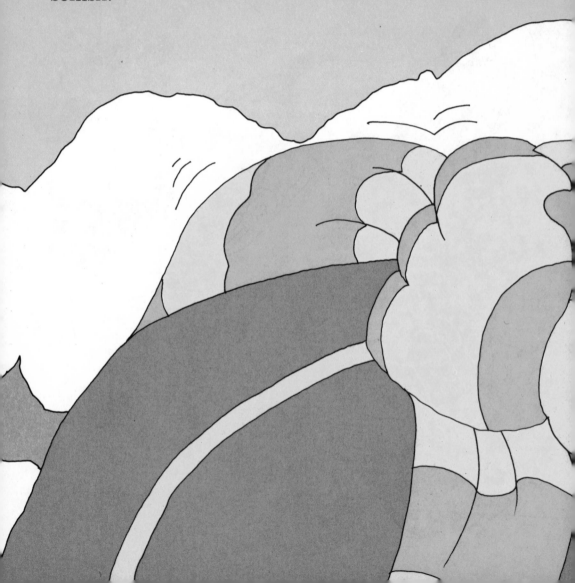

Walrus got to Bear's door. "You would think that
after all I've done for him, he'd lend me one little hat
to keep my poor head warm. Oh, no!" screeched
Walrus. "Not Bear. He's too mean to lend a measly
hat to his best friend. He wants the starter's job for
himself! He doesn't care if I go out in the cold and
get sick! Some friend!"

Walrus pounded on Bear's door. "I'll tell him what I think of him!" Bear opened the door and smiled. "YOU CAN KEEP YOUR ROTTEN HAT!" screamed Walrus.

Walrus turned away and marched off down the street.

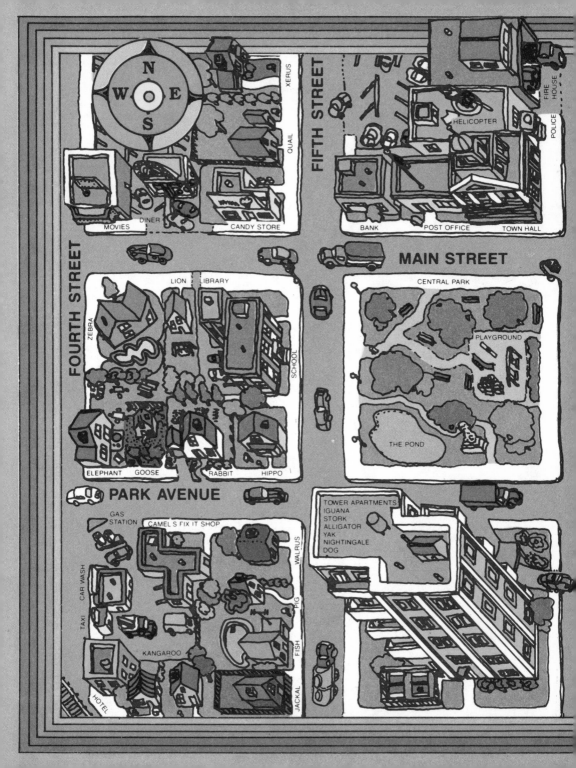